218636

4-6-11

D1609303

You Can't Milk VOID a Dancing Cow

By Tom Dunsmuir
Illustrated by Brian T. Jones

Tanglewood Press
Terre Haute, Indiana

Published by Tanglewood Press, LLC, October 2005.

Book and text design by Amy Alick Perich.

Tanglewood Press, LLC
P. O. Box 3009
Terre Haute, IN 47803
www.tanglewoodbooks.com

Printed in the United States of America

10 9 8 7 6 5 4 4 3 2 1

ISBN 0-9749303-3-4
    978-0-9749303-3-6

One rainy spring, Farmer Picket's wife made five pairs of overalls with her new sewing machine.

"Thank you dear, I have enough overalls now," said Farmer Picket.

"Then I have an idea," said Mrs. Picket. And she made three cow-sized raincoats. She sent Farmer Picket to town to buy six pairs of boots.

The cows were so happy, they refused to come inside to be milked.

"I'm glad the rainy season is over," Farmer Picket said when summer came.
"Summer is so hot," said Mrs. Picket. "I have an idea."
She made bonnets for the chickens. She sent Farmer Picket to town to buy a flock of sunglasses.

All summer, the chickens paraded in their outfits instead of laying eggs.

"I'm glad summer is over," said Farmer Picket on the first day of fall.
     But Mrs. Picket saw the rooster shiver in the morning chill. "I have an idea,"
she said. She made the rooster flannel pajamas and a nightcap.

The rooster was so comfy-cozy,
he slept in.

So did Farmer Picket!

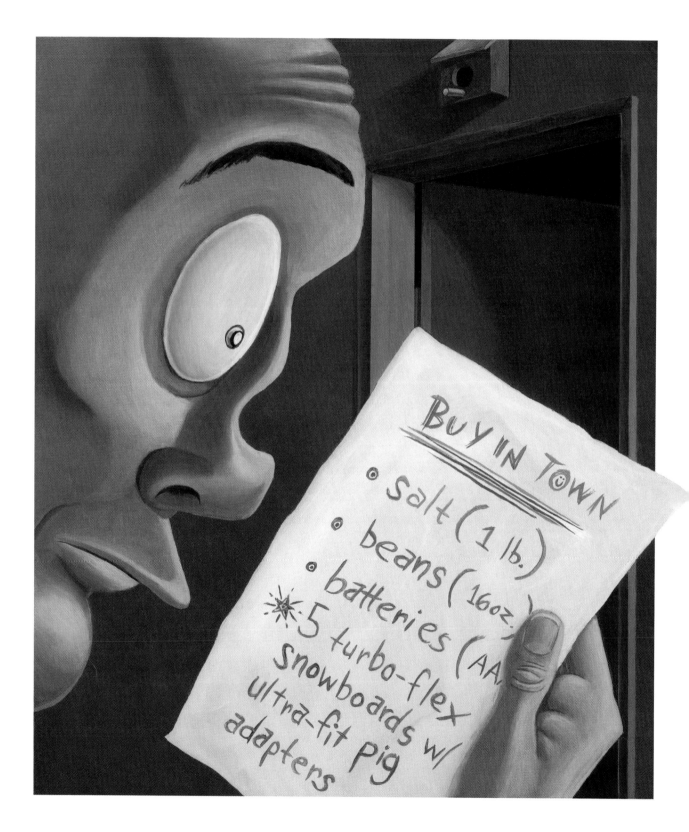

Farmer Picket had just celebrated the end of fall when his wife had a new idea. She sewed five snowsuits for the pigs. She sent Farmer Picket to town to buy five snowboards.

That winter the pigs got so much exercise, they lost weight.
"How do I sell skinny pigs?" Farmer Picket complained.

When spring arrived, Mrs. Picket said, "I have another idea."
"The horses would look adorable in Hawaiian outfits."

The farmer sighed and drove to town for two paper leis.

The next morning, he plowed his field and listened to his boom box. Tess and Tina danced the hula down one row and up the other. "No more!" Farmer Picket huffed. "Mrs. Picket must stop sewing for the animals!"

When he got home, he found Mrs. Picket with her toolbox.
Her sewing machine was broken. "It can't be fixed," she sighed.

"I'll get you something better," Farmer Picket said.
He bought a computer in town.

"It doesn't sew," said Mrs. Picket. "But I have an idea…"

Weeks later, Farmer Picket almost drove off the road.
He'd spotted a llama wearing a tennis outfit.

"I have a surprise for you!" said Mrs. Picket the second he got home. Tacked on her wall were animal clothing designs she'd made on her computer. "I'm selling designs to the other farms," she said.

"I'm proud of you," Farmer Picket told her. "Your sewing machine gave up, but you didn't."

Mrs. Picket gave Farmer Picket a big kiss on his sunburned nose. "I have an idea," she said.

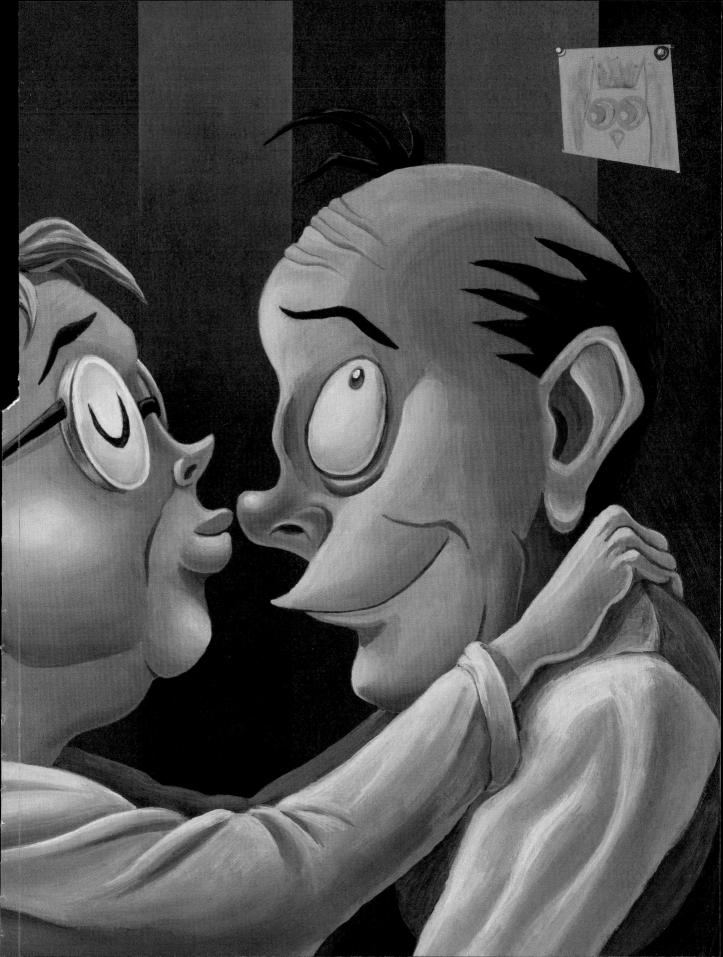